GW01316356

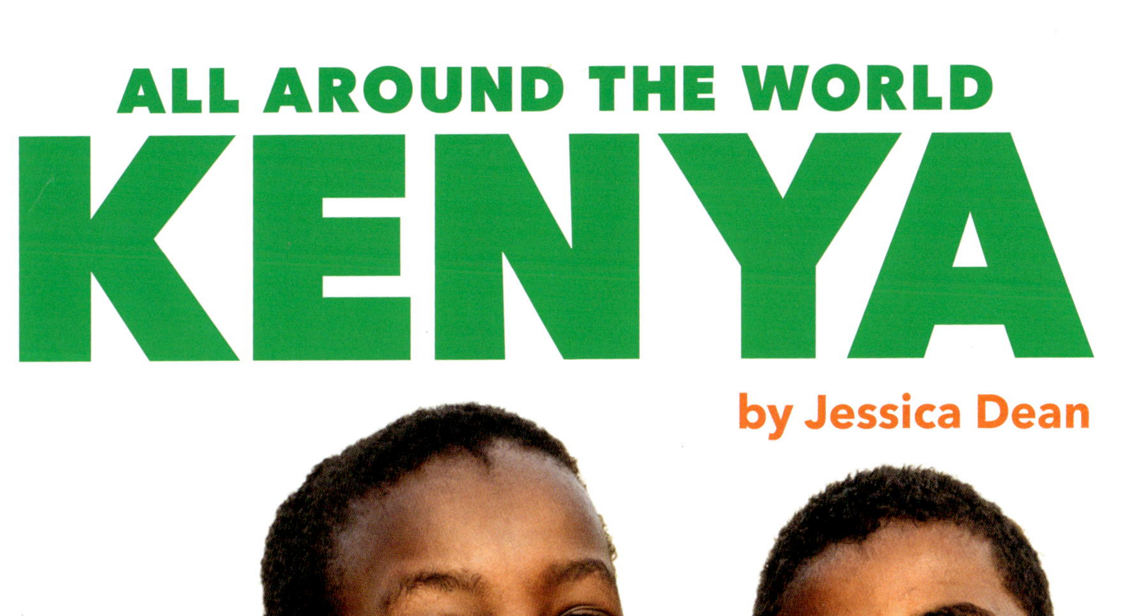

ALL AROUND THE WORLD

KENYA

by Jessica Dean

Ideas for Parents and Teachers

Pogo Books let children practice reading informational text while introducing them to nonfiction features such as headings, labels, sidebars, maps, and diagrams, as well as a table of contents, glossary, and index.

Carefully leveled text with a strong photo match offers early fluent readers the support they need to succeed.

Before Reading

- "Walk" through the book and point out the various nonfiction features. Ask the student what purpose each feature serves.
- Look at the glossary together. Read and discuss the words.

Read the Book

- Have the child read the book independently.
- Invite him or her to list questions that arise from reading.

After Reading

- Discuss the child's questions. Talk about how he or she might find answers to those questions.
- Prompt the child to think more. Ask: The annual wildebeest migration takes place in Kenya. Are you able to see animals migrate where you live?

Pogo Books are published by Jump!
5357 Penn Avenue South
Minneapolis, MN 55419
www.jumplibrary.com

Library of Congress Cataloging-in-Publication Data

Names: Dean, Jessica, 1963- author.
Title: Kenya / by Jessica Dean.
Description: Minneapolis : Jump!, [2019]
Series: All around the world
"Pogo Books are published by Jump!" | Includes index.
Identifiers: LCCN 2018023790 (print)
LCCN 2018032093 (ebook)
ISBN 9781641281690 (ebook)
ISBN 9781641281676 (hardcover : alk. paper)
ISBN 9781641281683 (pbk.)
Subjects: LCSH: Kenya–Juvenile literature.
Classification: LCC DT433.522 (ebook)
LCC DT433.522 .D44 2019 (print) | DDC 967.62–dc23
LC record available at https://lccn.loc.gov/2018023790

Editor: Kristine Spanier
Designer: Molly Ballanger

Photo Credits: Volodymyr Burdiak/Shutterstock, cover; Bartosz Hadyniak/iStock, 1, 12-13, 14-15; Pixfiction/Shutterstock, 3; KA Photography KEVM111/Shutterstock, 4; WanderingNomad/iStock, 5; matthieu Gallet/Shutterstock, 6tl; Daleen Loest/Shutterstock, 6-7t; EcoPrint/Shutterstock, 6bl; JMx Images/Shutterstock, 6-7b; Kirill Dorofeev/Shutterstock, 8-9; Sopotnicki/Shutterstock, 10; Peter Groenendijk/robertharding/SuperStock, 11; stanislaff/Shutterstock, 16; Emma Kadenyi Ombima/Shutterstock, 17; Bloomberg/Getty, 18-19; Paul Gilham/Getty, 20-21; Anton_Ivanov/Shutterstock, 23.

Printed in the United States of America at Corporate Graphics in North Mankato, Minnesota.

TABLE OF CONTENTS

CHAPTER 1
Welcome to Kenya! 4

CHAPTER 2
Kenya's People 10

CHAPTER 3
Life in Kenya 16

QUICK FACTS & TOOLS
At a Glance 22
Glossary 23
Index 24
To Learn More 24

CHAPTER 1

WELCOME TO KENYA!

See lions sleeping in the sun. Visit the people of a **native tribe**. Go bird-watching. Welcome to Kenya!

It is warm year-round here. Spring and fall bring heavy rains. **Deserts** remain dry. Mount Kenya is high enough to have snow at the top!

gazelle
Cape buffalo

yellow baboon

cheetah

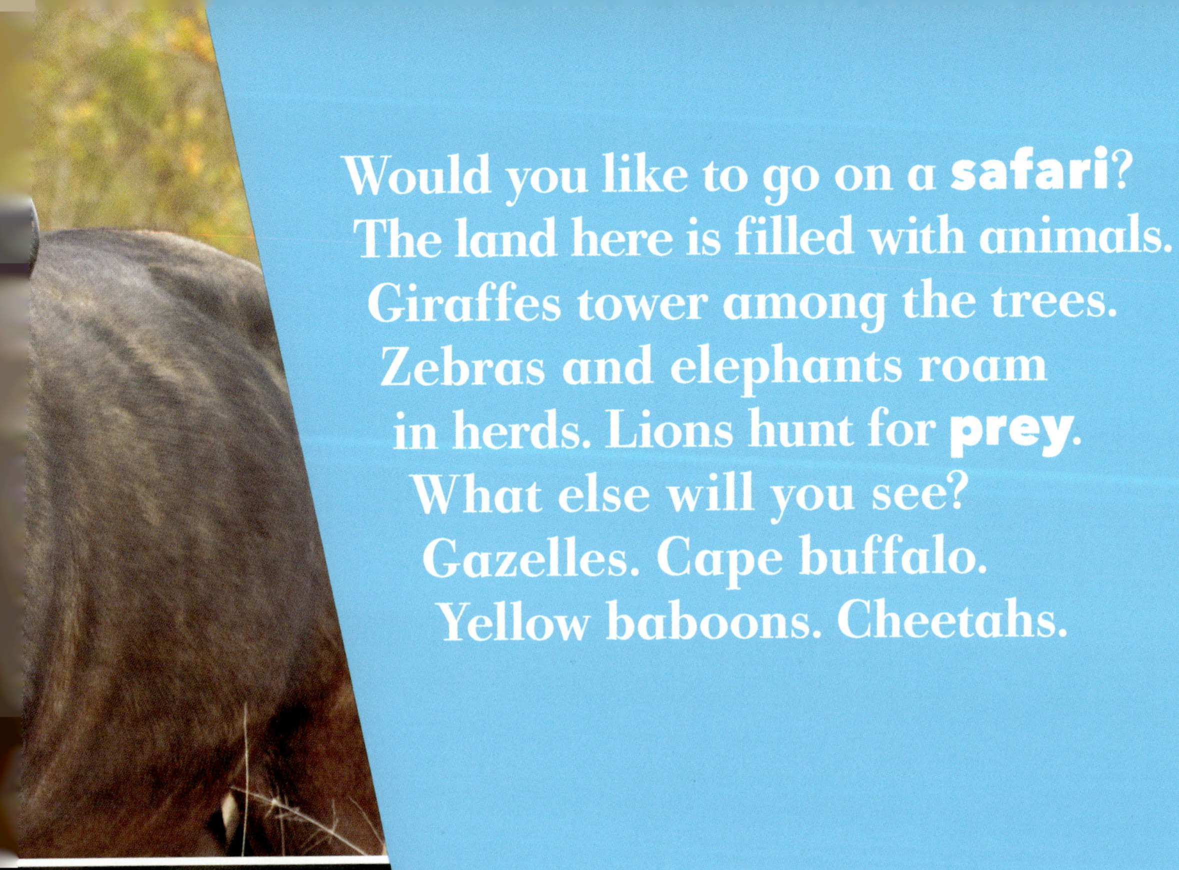

Would you like to go on a **safari**? The land here is filled with animals. Giraffes tower among the trees. Zebras and elephants roam in herds. Lions hunt for **prey**. What else will you see? Gazelles. Cape buffalo. Yellow baboons. Cheetahs.

Lake Nakuru is known as a soda lake. Why? It has high levels of salt in it. More than 500 different kinds of birds are here. The flamingo is one. The blue-eared starling is another. Black rhinos and warthogs live here, too.

DID YOU KNOW?

The Great Rift Valley is nearby. This split in Earth's **crust** runs south through Africa. It has an average width of 30 to 40 miles (48 to 64 kilometers).

CHAPTER 2

KENYA'S PEOPLE

Kenya's **capital** is Nairobi. It is filled with **skyscrapers**. More than four million people live here.

Outdoor markets are popular. People can shop for handmade crafts. Jewelry. Décor. Clothing.

Many different **ethnic** groups live in Kenya. Many still practice their traditional lifestyles. Women make colorful bead necklaces. Men participate in jumping dances. Each one leaps as high as he can. This shows strength.

TAKE A LOOK!

The beaded necklaces of the Maasai women are an important part of the tribe's **culture**. The colors of the beads stand for different values.

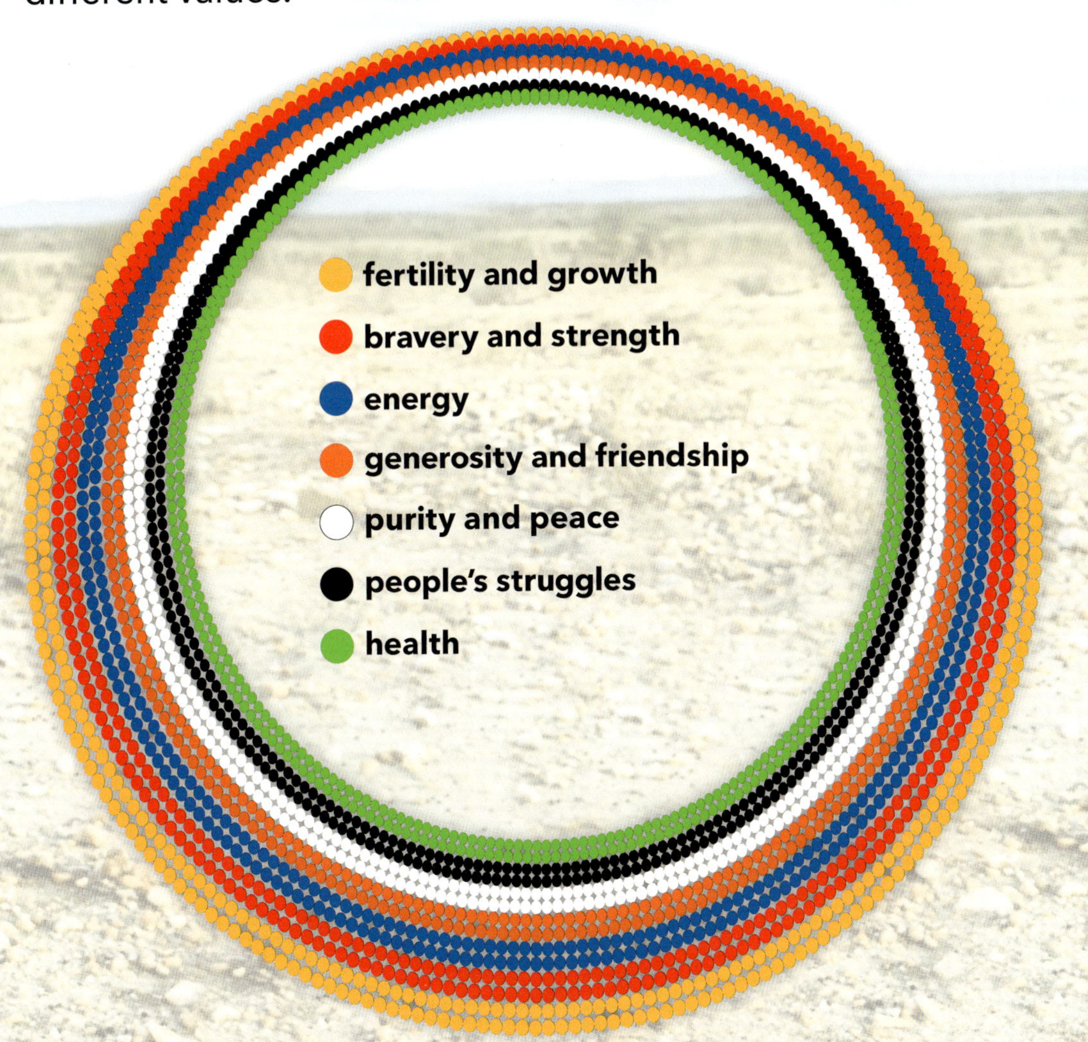

Kids attend school from ages 6 to 14. Students learn English. This helps people from different tribes communicate. Children must pass difficult exams to enter high school.

Many families grow just enough food to feed the family. How do kids help out? They may plant seeds. Help with cattle. Or fetch water. Bigger farms grow coffee. Tea. Flowers. These **crops** are **exports**.

WHAT DO YOU THINK?

Music is an important part of the culture here. Children learn to sing and play drums at a young age. Do you know how to play an instrument? If not, do you want to learn?

CHAPTER 3

LIFE IN KENYA

Many people do not have refrigerators here. They eat fresh produce. Like what? Pineapples. Bananas. Green vegetables. They also eat food made of grains and other ingredients that don't **spoil**.

Christmas is a special day for many Kenyans. A feast called nyama choma is served. This is grilled goat or beef. It is served with ugali, a bread made from ground corn. Families go to church and sing carols.

Jubilee
Tuko Pamoja

Jamhuri Day marks the day British rule ended in 1963. It falls on December 12. Parades and speeches take place. People watch the Jamhuri Day Cup. It is an important soccer tournament.

Some of the world's best distance runners come from Kenya. They have won many races and Olympic medals. People here also like to play rugby and cricket.

Kenya is an amazing country. Would you like to visit?

WHAT DO YOU THINK?

A favorite game here is called mancala. Two players race to capture stones from holes on a board. What games do you play with your family?

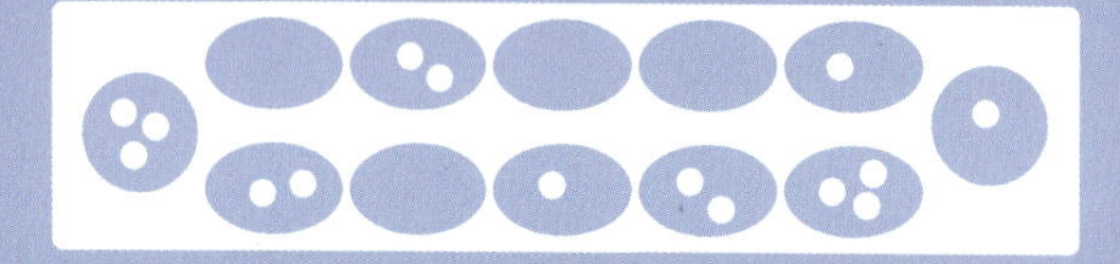

KENYA
Rio2016
RUDISHA

QUICK FACTS & TOOLS

AT A GLANCE

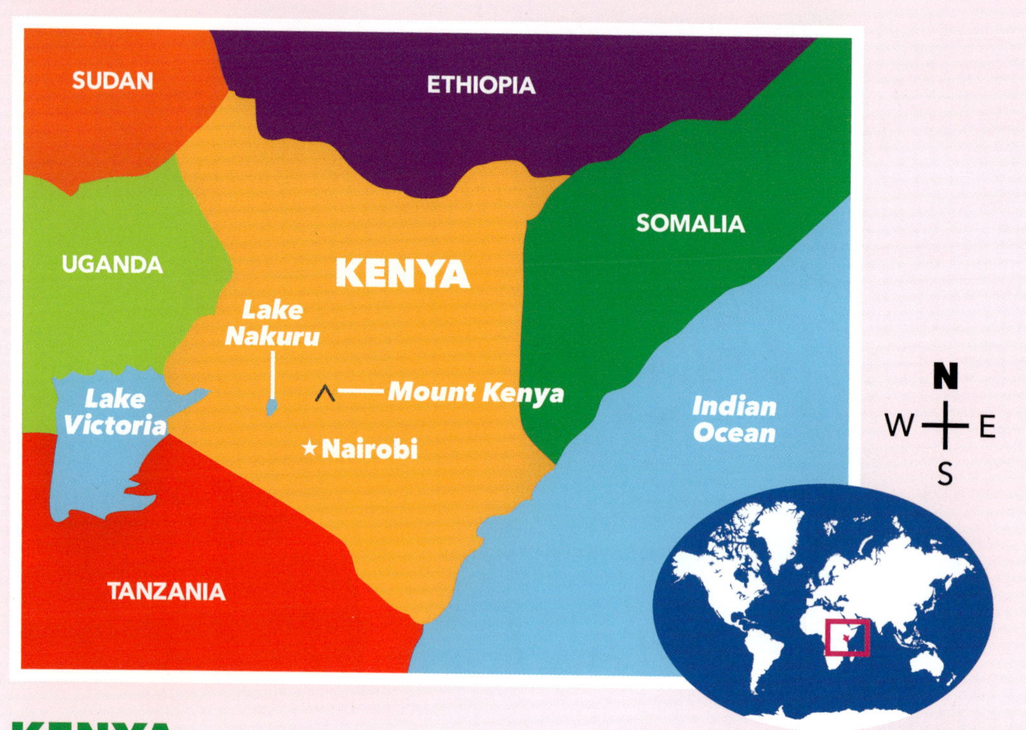

KENYA

Location: East Africa

Size: 224,081 square miles (580,367 square kilometers)

Population: 47,615,739 (July 2017 estimate)

Capital: Nairobi

Type of Government: presidential republic

Languages: English and Kiswahili

Exports: tea, flowers, coffee, petroleum products

Currency: Kenyan shilling

GLOSSARY

capital: A city where government leaders meet.

crops: Plants grown for food.

crust: The hard outer layer of Earth.

culture: The ideas, customs, traditions, and ways of life of a group of people.

deserts: Dry areas where hardly any plants grow because there is so little rain.

ethnic: Of or having to do with a group of people sharing the same national origins, language, or culture.

exports: Products sold to different countries.

native: Having been born in a particular country or place.

prey: Animals that are hunted by other animals for food.

safari: A trip taken, especially in Africa, to see large wild animals.

skyscrapers: Very tall buildings.

spoil: To become rotten or unfit for eating.

tribe: A large group of related people who share the same language, customs, and laws, and who usually live in the same area.

Kenya's currency

INDEX

animals 4, 7, 8
bead necklaces 12, 13
Christmas 17
crops 15
culture 13, 15
deserts 5
ethnic groups 12
exports 15
food 15, 16, 17
Great Rift Valley 8
Jamhuri Day 19
Jamhuri Day Cup 19
Lake Nakuru 8
Maasai 13
mancala 20
markets 11
Mount Kenya 5
music 15
Nairobi 10
runners 20
safari 7
school 15
skyscrapers 10
tribes 4, 13, 15

TO LEARN MORE

Learning more is as easy as 1, 2, 3.

1) Go to www.factsurfer.com
2) Enter "Kenya" into the search box.
3) Click the "Surf" button to see a list of websites.

With factsurfer, finding more information is just a click away.